I0712798

ROO KING.

RAY SYNIGAL

ACKNOWLEDGMENTS

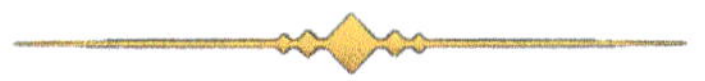

Thanks to everyone who helped me to create my
book, Sidney Stuckett (Editor from Upwork),
Web Design Technicians for my Book Cover . . .

Let's keep Inspiring Others And Making Our
World A Much Better Place By Unleashing
More Positivity!

Stop The Hate, and Spread Love!

DEDICATION

For the people I know who encouraged me

on my Publishing Journey

and for those who are craving

some new Hope and Faith

after the Pandemic.

TABLE OF CONTENTS

CHAPTER 1
The Beginning

On a nice cool Friday night in December 1997 , in the deep south of the deadly Louisiana swamps, a clan of 8 huge Omega Werewolves were traveling on the dark Louisiana road of Hwy 51 in Laplace, with one of the werewolves being a baby.

Although the baby brown werewolf was just born, it was already hunting deer with the rest of the Omega Werewolves.

The Omega Werewolves spotted a group of deer and chased them. After the Male Omega Leader Werewolf caught a deer each for both his female mate and his 5 foot baby brown werewolf, one of the baby deer was brutally eaten by the brown baby werewolf to help him grow.

The Omega Werewolves knew that this brown pup was not only very special but a chosen one.

However, a couple of slender, white kaiju scientists with blond hair named Jeff Segal and Oscar Caesar, who were also ex-MMA Fighters, worked at a massive scientific and military kaiju base in New Orleans known as Alpha/Omega X in December of 1997. Jeff wears glasses while Oscar doesn't.

"What the hell is making that noise in the swamp?" said Jeff.

In December 1997, Jeff discovered that in the dark and deadly Louisiana swamps, there was a clan of Werewolves that lived back there. He saw that they had a brown, werewolf pup. He went to tell his boss, Stephen Hancock, who was also the founder of Alpha/Omega X, that there was a clan of Werewolves in the swamps of Louisiana on Hwy 51 in Laplace. However, Stephen didn't believe him. So, he decided to go take a ride to the swamps himself, and to his surprise, he saw them, especially the brown werewolf.

It was at this point that Stephen realized Jeff was right about the Omega Werewolf Clan living in the swamp. Unfortunately, when Stephen headed back to Alpha/Omega X, he immediately wanted a special weapon made.

Stephen wanted them to make a special weapon called Ultanium. He began to explain how he wanted it to look and how powerful he wanted it to be for his scientists.

Stephen planned to make kaijus all over the globe by expanding his kaiju scientific company. Once the scientists got a grasp on what he wanted the Ultanium to look like, which was Red Smoke filled with something powerful inside it to make animals in the swamp and the lake turn into kaijus, the scientists realized this was a super dangerous experiment, and that they must take extra precautions to make sure the first experiment goes smoothly.

Also, for his scientist's second project, Stephen wanted them to create missiles filled with Ultanium so he could send his military to drop the Ultanium Missiles on the Louisiana swamps and lakes.

Three years later in December of 2000, Jeff went back to the Louisiana Swamps after his laboratory shift to study the Omega Werewolves Clan up close.

He got out of his small, green Chevrolet truck with no weapons and spotted the Clan of Omega Werewolves from a distance. He also spotted the Brown Werewolf pup got huge. He was very surprised by how big the pup grew within 3 years. Jeff thinks the baby Brown Werewolf is now 9'7 feet tall.

The next day, Jeff went back to Alpha/Omega X, and the Ultanium missiles were finally ready to launch. Stephen wanted his Alpha/Omega X elite military troops to send the missiles to the Swamps, but Jeff was against that decision. Stephen and Jeff got into a big argument about sending the missiles to the swamps.

Surprisingly, they heard something loud outside and looked out of the window. At first, they didn't see anything, but moments later they saw an Enormous Black Spider with White Wings coming down from the sky and heading for the swamp. Because of this, Jeff and Stephen put their differences aside and discovered that the Spider was not from Earth. Stephen called it the Space Spider Kaiju, while Jeff called it the Alien Spider Kaiju.

In the Swamp, on a different dark and cool night, the Enormous Space-Alien Spider Kaiju landed where the Werewolves were, which led to a big battle.

The 9 ft 7 inches tall Brown Werewolf looked at the big battle from a distance, feeling both powerless and depressed that he couldn't destroy that Space-Alien Spider with Wings. All he could do was watch as the Omega Werewolf Clan fought a great fight. Unfortunately, in the end, the giant Space-Alien Spider destroyed them all in combat. From a distance on the shoulder of Louisiana Hwy 51 Road, The Brown Beast witnessed the destruction in both fury and sadness.

Ex-MMA Fighter and Kaiju Scientist, Oscar Caesar, showed up and saw the Brown Beast and he tried to connect with him. After a while, the Brown Beast ended up feeling a deep connection with him.

However, Alpha/Omega X ended up showing up in their vehicle moments later. Jeff tried reaching out to them while The Brown Beast protected Oscar from Alpha/Omega X.

Fortunately, The Brown Beast knew Jeff was a great guy too, much like Oscar, so he did not hurt him. However, when Stephen arrived, he felt a very negative vibe and wanted to kill The Brown Beast for some strange reasons, which caused The Brown Beast to flee.

Two days later, Stephen ordered his military troops to send out missiles with Ultanium to the Swamp. First, the 3 AOX military troops geared up and then prepared to load the Ultanium Missiles onto their jets.

Next, AOX military troops on three jets were loading the missiles into their jets for launch. A few moments later, after they got on their jets to prepare for launch, Stephen ordered them to take off immediately.

The three AOX Military Jet Fighters were flying super-fast but with amazing accuracy and precision.

While the jets were on their way, the Brown Werewolf was looking after his dead relatives. Suddenly, a big Black Snake came out of the water while being depressed by his tragic family death. Against his will, the Brown Werewolf ended up fighting the snake. Fortunately, the Brown Werewolf won, but the Black Snake was not dead.

Although it was still moving, the Black Snake went on its way after testing the Brown Werewolf. Unfortunately, before the Black Snake could leave, three AOX Jet Fighters ended up dropping one of their big missiles on the Black Snake and the Brown Werewolf in the Swamp.

A big explosion of Ultanium quickly spreads and within minutes, the Swamp was covered in tons of Ultanium. The Brown Werewolf and the other creatures had either passed out or were dying from the deadly chemicals in the red smoke.

The Ultanium killed off a lot of animals like alligators, fish, raccoons, possums, and many more. However, a new UIC (UnIdentified Creature) lizard was exposed to the Ultanium in the water as the Ultanium spread to Lake Pontchartrain as well.

With the spreading of the gas, lots of changes occurred in the deadly swamps of Louisiana that day.

21 years later, in January of 2021, Oscar and Jeff wanted to head back to the Swamps to see what had happened since then. To see if there was still life there. Oscar had a gut feeling that something had happened to his friend, the Brown Werewolf in the swamp. He wanted to go visit the swamp as he felt that the world had changed since the coronavirus pandemic took place. Jeff agreed with his long-time co-worker, Oscar. Also, Oscar was very unhappy with the police brutality that had been going

on and was so glad that Joe Biden and Kamala Harris would be the President and Vice President.

However, he didn't think that was enough Hope and Faith to rebuild the USA for the better. He felt that the US needed something enormous to make a change in the world, to help humanity finally come together.

Jeff agreed that bad humans especially, bad cops, deserved the death penalty. He wanted more justice and peace in the country, he also thought it was going to take something massive to solve the problem in the world and give humanity a much better chance at Unity and Peace once and for all, instead of trying to divide and conquer other ethnicities.

Jeff and Oscar let Stephen know that they were going on an expedition back to the swamp to discover what was left. They had a feeling that something had happened and that the swamp could have evolved.

Surprisingly, Stephen didn't care if they went, or not, as long as they did not include him in case something went south. They agreed and soon, on a Friday Afternoon in January, Jeff and Oscar went on an adventure back to the swamp.

Amazingly, they were both super nervous even though Jeff was driving. Oscar was feeling goosebumps in his belly and through his gut at the thought that the swamp had evolved.

As they were passing on the Lake Pontchartrain bridge to Laplace, they saw a fog ahead, so they couldn't really tell if the swamp had evolved or not.

Even after they exited the bridge and headed to the swamp on Hwy 51, they still saw some fog. However, it was not like the fog on the bridge.

Surprisingly, they still saw a little bit of the Ultanium in the swamp, which meant that the swamp had evolved to some degree. Jeff and Oscar got out of their truck on the shoulder of Hwy 51 and went to the same place they were 21 years ago. There they saw the Brown Werewolf's Family's Bones lined up on the shoulder of the road in the swamp's grass.

Jeff thought the Brown Werewolf was dead after the Ultanium explosion, but Oscar had a feeling it wasn't dead. Interestingly, Oscar heard that something colossal was coming their way by way of huge stomps. Both Jeff and Oscar agreed that a giant monster was coming their way. Moments later, they saw the giant beast and it was the Brown Werewolf. Although Oscar was right, both he and Jeff were very surprised. The Giant Brown Werewolf saw them and went over to them. Fortunately, he remembered them even though it had been a little over two decades since he last saw the humans. Overjoyed, Oscar gave him a weird, but awesome kaiju, and gladiator, named, ROO KING.

He gave the Brown Wolf this name because Oscar believed he was a King. ROO KING's long pointy ears, with his long black claws and his Omega scars on his face give him a very unique, monstrous appearance. Even Jeff actually liked the name Oscar came up with.

ROO KING felt the same connection with the two humans as he did before. However, their reunion was cut short as ROO KING heard something close by in the swamp. ROO KING protected the two humans by fighting the giant black serpent, SERPO.

The False King of the Louisiana Swamp now fought his new threat, ROO KING, for the kingdom. SERPO and ROO KING got into a big fight in the Swamp. SERPO tried to wrap him up in a snake choke and bite him with his enormous mouth and super large white teeth.

ROO KING showed his super large white teeth too and had his right hand on SERPO'S throat and his other hand scratching him brutally with his enormously sharp, long, brownish claws. However, SERPO was not fazed by the huge scratch and started to fight dirty by spitting his super deadly red acid to get ROO KING off him, and it worked. ROO KING was severely hurt by the red acid, which was his weakness.

SERPO fought dirty again and quickly bit ROO KING in his left shoulder and hit ROO KING with his super sharp red acid-end tail. He started stabbing ROO KING in his chest causing him to feel super weak and then he collapsed.

Jeff and Oscar watched the big fight from a distance, recording it. Oscar hated the enormous SERPO and both of them agreed that SERPO was the False King of the Louisiana Swamps.

Oscar was feeling hurt and hopeless but Jeff saw something that looked like Dark Orange light up from the Monstrous Brown Werewolf's eyes that gave SERPO a run for his money.

Oscar believed ROO KING'S Dark Orange Omega laser beams were extremely powerful. Unfortunately, ROO KING missed and SERPO brutally bit him in his right shoulder to finish the fight. ROO KING yelped loudly in pain. SERPO, the False King of Louisiana Swamps won the big fight wickedly and tried to go after Jeff and Oscar, but Oscar came prepared by shooting at SERPO. SERPO was angry.

Hissing loudly, he decided to leave but tried to brutally tail-whip them as he left. In the end, SERPO ended up flying somewhere, but Jeff and Oscar had no idea where. However, the sky looked more and more cloudy as it got darker in the afternoon.

Fortunately, ROO KING was able to get up and went for a walk to Lake Pontchartrain to drink his water in order to help him heal. Oscar and Jeff followed ROO KING to the lake. They thought that ROO KING could be what the world needed in a deadly time with the coronavirus pandemic, that he could restore Hope and Faith for not just the people in Louisiana but for people all over the world. He was that Big Faith during this Pandemic.

Later, at night, back in NOLA, Oscar met a young Mexican Woman named Astrid Rodriguez, who was a Pharmacist and a filmmaker. Astrid does filmmaking as a side hustle outside of being a Pharmacist. Astrid and Oscar both felt a connection with each other after he told her that he was a Kaiju Scientist and an ex-MMA Fighter.

Astrid told him that she loves martial arts and monsters. Oscar was very shocked that she loved monsters. On the other hand, Jeff and Astrid met each other but they both didn't feel a connection.

Later, a twenty-two-year-old Black Man named Tyrone McStevens was jogging in the street and a car was honking at him. Oscar immediately went over to save him from the car. Tyrone thanked him for saving his life.

"I'm very upset and depressed by being rejected by girls on Snapchat and by meeting girls every time I try to talk to them in person," Tyrone said to Oscar.

"I think it's better if you move on and don't give up looking for the right girl, to keep looking for the right one for you," Oscar replied.

"Hey kid, how would you like to come work for us at AOX in the city?" said Oscar.

"Hmm, I would, but what is AOX?" Tyrone replied. Oscar explained to him what AOX meant.

"I figure you would say that haha. It stands for Alpha/Omega X. We study Kaijus/Gladiators and we have a big military base here in the city and it will be nice for you to come check out our super advanced scientific and military facility."

"Woah that is awesome, I'm in for sure," said Tyrone with enthusiasm. Jeff didn't think it was right to go work at AOX during a pandemic, or in general. Oscar ignored Jeff and got Tyrone into the Super Kaiju Laboratory.

Tyrone would much rather be in the Super Kaiju facility than be in college, and most certainly in Quarantine at home, bored just thinking about his very painful past experiences with girls on both social media and real life. Astrid and Tyrone met with some great excitement and super positivity. Astrid gave him some pointers on girls for future reference.

"Pleasure to meet you, Tyrone, just be yourself and whoever doesn't like you for you, is their loss. You truly deserve better, you seem like a very cool guy. I'm sorry that has happened to you," said Astrid as everyone headed to the Super Kaiju Laboratory at AOX.

Oscar drove them to the facility to show Tyrone and Astrid the AOX Grand Facility in New Orleans. Once they showed up at the facility, Astrid and Tyrone were very intrigued with how epic it looked with the capturing design of the Company Logo and how amazingly colorful it also was.

While on their tour of the facility, Astrid and Tyrone were speechless. Likewise, once they entered the Super Kaiju lab, they were even more excited and couldn't believe how extraordinary the Kaiju AOX Facility really was.

"Woah, what is this book, it's humongous?" Astrid said, pointing out a huge brown book in the lab on the experiment table. Jeff told her what the book was about.

"That book is called The Ultimate Kaiju History Book from as far back as the 15th Century.

"In it are the majority of the kaijus from today that we may encounter, and it has the origins of the kaijus in it too," said Jeff with some pride. Oscar ended up taking everyone home before it got too late.

He gave Tyrone a chance to come and work with them to help him better his life. Fortunately, everyone made it home safe for the night.

Oscar and Jeff woke up when it was dawn, ate breakfast, and made it to the lab. In the lab, on a very cloudy morning, AOX experienced consistent Lake Disturbance activity from Lake Pontchartrain and as time went on, the disturbance activity was getting a lot faster and stronger.

Stephen wanted to send his scientific crew down by the lake to see if that was a waterspout, or if there was something enormous in the water.

However, instead of sending his crew out by the lake, he sent a special big AOX Black Designed Drone that had a special camera system and an incredible creature tracker in it as well to give AOX Scientists information of a kaiju if there was one in the lake.

Surprisingly, Tyrone and Astrid showed up at the scientific lab. Oscar was excited and stunned to see them back in the lab.

"I'm so glad y'all could make it. We are tracking Lake Pontchartrain in Kenner to see if there is a kaiju in the water," said Oscar.

Stephen met Tyrone and Astrid in a surprisingly good mood but did not really want them there. The drone took a picture of ROO KING from a distance in the lake going back to the swamp.

Stephen was super shocked that the Brown Beast was still living and was now an extremely powerful colossal Brown Beast.

However, the wave activity was ROO KING walking in the lake. Interestingly, ROO KING seemed to be tracking something in the lake from the image of the pic where he was facing the lake from the swamp and interestingly, another image showed ROO KING looking up at the sky angry with his fists balled up.

In conclusion, his huge teeth showing and blasting his Dark Orange Omega Beams at full speed and brute force from his eyes, looking at the sky that he felt was a big threat. ROO KING felt threatened by something that was in the air coming down to Earth, close to his area.

CHAPTER 2
Rise/Battle of the Giant Beasts

Oscar felt like there was something in the air coming to Earth that ROO KING saw as a big threat to humanity. However, a big alarm went off at AOX to warn them that the kaiju was rising.

Everyone saw a new image of what was in Lake Pontchartrain; it was a giant blue and whitish three-legged lizard with light green eyes. Fortunately, he was on ROO KING'S side by also rising and feeling a massive threat was coming to Earth. Oscar knew the name of the creature and described him.

"Oh snap, that creature is not an Unidentified Creature, the real name of the creature is called The LakeCrawler and it is the King Of The Lakes and Oceans. The ancient tribes called him THE OCEAN REAPER in the Ultimate Kaiju History Book.

I'm so surprised it is still living as it is definitely one of the oldest kaijus in the book," said Oscar while being very intrigued by The Lake Crawler. Oscar believed that this Lake Crawler was the last of his kind.

Stephen wanted to kill all of the kaijus to reclaim Earth for humanity. However, Jeff, Oscar, Tyrone, and Astrid totally disagreed with him.

"I will kill all of them to take back our planet. Earth belongs to humans, not some stupid giant monsters," said Stephen with some rage.

Jeff and everyone strongly disagreed with him.

"Sir, you can't kill these awesome creatures. They are a part of Earth and connected to this planet just as much as humans," said Jeff.

"Sir, the truth is Earth belongs to the gladiators. This is their planet. I read it in the Kaiju Ultimate History Book. Killing them will bring chaos to the planet," said Oscar. Stephen still wanted to destroy all of the kaijus despite everyone disagreeing with him.

He ordered his AOX military troops to create a powerful enough weapon to destroy all of the kaijus/gladiators. Jeff was looking to stop them in any way. Not to mention, they were looking at their super-advanced Earth globe in the lab seeing movements from around the world. Oscar broke down in detail the Super Earth Globe Technology.

"The name of the technology we are using is called THE KAIJUNIZER. It's a super advanced Earth globe kaiju machine that can track any kaiju images, anatomy, sounds, history, and movement speeds, and can have control of all the kaijus from around the globe. Be very careful.

"Anything we want to know about the kaijus we are dealing with is here. Welcome to the future of kaijus on Earth! Not to mention it can also track if some kaijus on Earth are pretending to be from Earth but really aren't." Oscar went into detail about the different abilities THE KAIJUNIZER had over the kaijus around the world.

The threat that ROO KING was looking at from the drone image were two very weird-looking colossal monsters that weren't from Earth, which caused THE KAIJUNIZER to go on a Severe Alert to warn everyone of what was coming.

"Whoa, that is a gigantic, evil, whitish worm with red eyes and oh snap, that's a giant black spider with white wings! This is insane and it looks like they are causing the Earth kaijus to be awakened and rise," said Tyrone with curiosity.

THE KAIJUNIZER was Alpha/Omega X's Secret Weapon that they were secretly building to discover more about the different kaijus in the world. STORM MONGA and SPIDOTRON seemed to have a controlling effect on the kaijus on Earth causing them to rise from their habitats. Oscar and Jeff were very pleased and amazed with Tyrone's understanding of the kaijus uprising.

"Tyrone, I couldn't agree more with you. THE KAIJUNIZER tells us your theory is correct just as each of these other countries in different environments have the kaijus rising. Well done young man," said Jeff with some excitement.

Jeff agreed with Tyrone's thought on how the gigantic man-eating worm beast and the giant spider with wings monster were controlling the kaijus on Earth.
However, Oscar was thinking of something interesting and he had a feeling that ROO KING rose up to warn humanity about what was coming, but humans didn't listen to him.

"Guys, I finally understand now, you are right Tyrone, but I came up with a theory that what if ROO KING rises to warn us about these wicked monsters coming to Earth? Because guys look carefully in the picture where he was blasting his beams. "Notice he looked more disturbed than the image of when he was looking just at the LAKE MONSTER also known as THE LAKECRAWLER. Guys, I have a gut feeling ROO KING has warned us, but we didn't listen to him about the super danger that is coming to our planet," said Oscar with some concern.

Astrid thought Oscar might be right about this and now figured out why killing the kaijus would not be a good idea. Interestingly enough, more kaijus were appearing every second on THE KAIJUNIZER. Jeff went to warn Stephen about how killing the kaijus was now the worst idea.

Unfortunately, Stephen was not trying to listen and was still sending his troops into battle. Surprisingly, the drone hadn't been attacked by a kaiju/gladiator.

The drone was now showing ROO KING and THE LAKECRAWLER going into their epic battle against the monsters, SPIDOTRON and STORM MONGA, in Lake Pontchartrain on a very cloudy and dark day.

Unfortunately, a few moments later, SERPO flew over the lake and immediately bit down on ROO KING's left shoulder, squeezing him while STORM MONGA was getting the best of him. THE LAKECRAWLER then brutally bit off one of SPIDOTRON'S legs.

SPIDOTRON was severely hurt from the jaw strength and bite of THE LAKECRAWLER. Although THE LAKECRAWLER brutally ripped one of SPIDOTRON'S legs off, STORM MONGA jumped and brutally bit THE LAKECRAWLER. At the same time, ROO KING lit up SERPO with his Dark Orange Omega Beams and this time he didn't miss. He blasted SERPO severely, hurting him in the process.

SERPO immediately backed away from ROO KING just as SPIDOTRON'S leg quickly regenerated back. ROO KING charged at STORM MONGA while THE LAKECRAWLER was down regenerating. He was super hurt from STORM MONGA'S ferocious bite.

While Oscar and everyone were watching the big, brutal battle from the lab, Oscar, Astrid, and Tyrone decided to go watch them battle up close. Oscar started driving very fast just as Jeff went back into the scientist lab looking for everyone and finding no one. Astrid had THE KAIJUNIZER to truly test in person if the giant monsters were battling it out.

A few moments later, Oscar, Astrid, and Tyrone showed up at the battle. Astrid ended up testing THE KAIJUNIZER until she saw the AOX Military fighter jets come. AOX Military troops started shooting at the kaijus. STORM MONGA destroyed one of the AOX Jets as another big battle was unleashed at Lake Pontchartrain.

SPIDOTRON destroyed one of the fighter jets as well. Stephen used a few missiles at the kaijus. However, ROO KING demolished the missiles with the super powerful Dark Orange Omega Beams from his eyes at full blast and force.

ROO KING roared at the Jets. THE LAKECRAWLER jumped up and bit one of the jets by destroying it in one bite. The kaijus were surprisingly teaming up to take out the jets. Stephen realized Oscar and the others could have THE KAIJUNIZER, which made him highly upset.

Stephen regretted leaving THE KAIJUNIZER out in which he felt it was too powerful to be in another person's hands. Unfortunately for Stephen and his AOX Military troops, they were losing the battle. Stephen decided to pull his troops out of battle as STORM MONGA and SPIDOTRON both decided to fly away while SERPO stayed back and rematched with ROO KING.

Oscar saw SPIDOTRON and STORM MONGA fly away but didn't know where they were going. Meanwhile, ROO KING and SERPO were battling it out again.

SERPO regenerated and quickly went after him. SERPO spat out his red acid toward ROO KING.

ROO KING quickly dodged the vicious attack and brutally blasted at SERPO using his Dark Orange Omega Beams. This time, he caught SERPO and demolished him with his hands and claws by choking him and slamming him into the water.

SERPO ended up sneak attacking him and tried to viciously bite ROO KING. Surprisingly, THE LAKECRAWLER sneak attacked SERPO back by biting him with brute power.

"Wow, these were some incredible battles here today," said Tyrone with curiosity.

"You are so right Tyrone, these are some very interesting kaiju battles, however, this is just the beginning. War is coming," said Oscar.

Oscar believed that there were more kaiju fights on the way and that the lake battle was just a taste of what was coming. THE KAIJUNIZER went off as STORM MONGA and SPIDOTRON disappeared. Stephen finally realized that he needed another plan to take out the kaijus in order to save humanity.

Jeff disagreed with him, but he thought saving humanity was a priority in which he agreed with Stephen in that way of perspective. Jeff was looking at the kaiju map on AOX Tablet in the lab and more kaijus were rising around the world doing massive destruction and wreaking havoc in not only cities but in every country.

"Wait a second, what if these space gladiators were sent to Earth to destroy our planet, so they can rule the kaijus and destroy us all of humanity?" says Astrid out of fascination.

Oscar was thinking of a way to use THE KAIJUNIZER on the space kaijus to stop them from possibly destroying the planet at all costs no matter the risk. As Stephen and his military troops made it back to the AOX facility base, Jeff saw that the space monsters were on their way to New Orleans, flying slowly to possibly cause chaos in the city and humanity.

"Hey Oscar, y'all need to come back to the facility now. The gigantic, villainous space creatures are headed this way. Please come back to the lab, this is an emergency," says Jeff as he was concerned about the safety of the city before he called Oscar.

"Okay Jeff, we will be right there soon. We are coming now," said Oscar.

Oscar, Astrid, and Tyrone left Lake Pontchartrain to head back to the lab for safety. "I don't know if Oscar heading back to the lab is a bad idea. We should stay here. We're gonna be in danger going back to the lab," said Astrid in concern.   Tyrone didn't know what to believe. All he knew was that the kaijus were now rising and regaining their control of the planet. Oscar felt they should go back to the lab to warn others about the deadly creatures that were headed for the city. Surprisingly, STORM MONGA was creating storms while she was flying with her boo, SPIDOTRON. Apparently, they were a couple.

While Oscar was driving, Astrid and Tyrone tried to look for STORM MONGA and SPIDOTRON but they didn't know where they were. They thought they were in the sky way above the clouds where they could no longer be seen.

However, back at Lake Pontchartrain, SERPO hit THE LAKE CRAWLER with his red acid and THE LAKECRAWLER went down quickly.

ROO KING blasted him again with his Dark Orange Omega Beams, and this time he finally destroyed SERPO with the brute force of his super-powerful beams. SERPO went down in the water as ROO KING ended up howling, "OWOOOO" in his rematch victory against his enemy, SERPO.

Elsewhere, Oscar, Tyrone, and Astrid made it back to AOX Facility Base, but when they looked into the sky, they saw very dark black clouds slowly starting to form around NOLA.

In fact, after ROO KING howled, he looked towards New Orleans direction and saw that dark black, unusual clouds were starting to form. ROO KING got out of his orange rage and carefully looked at the big storm that was headed for New Orleans.

ROO KING decided to head back to the swamp and heal for a little while before going to the city. Meanwhile, Stephen introduced a new doctor to everyone whose name was Doctor Watkins.

Stephen trusted him to take over the company if something ended up happening to him. Jeff and Oscar found it very strange how Stephen could trust him when he didn't know him too well. Astrid had a bad feeling that Stephen was starting to betray AOX by not truly caring about the kaijus but trusting some strange Doctor who was supposed to be called a Kaiju Scientist when he already had two Kaiju Scientists.

The AOX Facility Emergency Alarm went off warning them a big kaiju storm was a mile away from the city. Surprisingly, that was not the kaiju storm but a regular storm.

The AOX Facility Base was a false alarm. STORM MONGA and SPIDOTRON were not anywhere to be found on the AOX Kaiju Tracker Monitor Tablet.

Stephen was very frustrated that he couldn't come up with a plan to stop the kaijus. He hated being wrong and always wanted to be right.

Amazingly, the AOX Kaiju Tracker started tracking two Monstrous Wasp Kaijus that were rising in the Louisiana Swamps and the Asian Giant Hornet Kaiju, rising from China, causing lots of chaos and destruction in Hong Kong.

"Something isn't right. Isn't it funny how all of these kaijus are rising and now two space kaiju are on Earth," said Tyrone, who was now curious if the space kaijus were somehow controlling the Earth Kaijus.

Tyrone knew something strange was happening to Mother Nature in the natural order making Jeff, Astrid, and Oscar seriously think over what Tyrone said. They concluded that it actually made sense.

Tyrone thought the Space Kaijus could be controlling the Earth Kaijus that were rising after they had arrived in the Earth's Stratosphere.

Controlling them to go against the natural order so that STORM MONGA and SPIDOTRON could possibly take over Earth easily.

Oscar thought he could be telling the truth and was trying to figure out why STORM MONGA and SPIDOTRON had come to Earth. Jeff was trying to think but the possibilities were endless as to why the Space Kaijus had come to the planet.

Meanwhile, Stephen was rethinking his combat strategy in his office against the kaijus to help him end them once and for all. He knew it was not going to be easy to take them out. He knew that he was going to need big, super-powerful weapons in order to have a chance against the giant beasts.

Unfortunately, STORM MONGA and SPIDOTRON had reappeared on the radar and they were coming pretty fast towards NOLA.

Astrid was beginning to have second thoughts about THE KAIJUNIZER they had brought with them to Lake Pontchartrain and that it may not have been THE REAL KAIJUNIZER.

Everything was starting to heat up as Space Kaijus continued to invade Earth. However, the coronavirus pandemic was still going on and even with a new virus, everyone forgot that they must wear a mask and sanitize everything so they can stop the spread of the virus.

Fortunately, AOX took extra precautions against the virus. Everyone was feeling down about the virus, especially with gigantic wicked space kaijus invading Earth.

The AOX Emergency Alarm went off as the villainous kaijus were now in the city and everyone was making their way to the AOX Secret Underground Basement for safety.

As night started, SERPO made it to New Orleans causing chaos in humanity and the city. Likewise, STORM MONGA and SPIDOTRON made it as well and reunited with SERPO. They then joined forces to destroy New Orleans as the storm began.

Fortunately, ROO KING had fully regenerated. He decided to leave the swamp and headed for New Orleans as he began to see an Orange Light in New Orleans which was really a big storm.

However, THE LAKE CRAWLER had also regenerated fully. ROO KING and THE LAKECRAWLER then teamed up as a powerful force to stop the villainous kaijus from destroying New Orleans.

They quickly headed for NOLA. ROO KING got into his Dark Orange Omega Beams Rage and THE LAKECRAWLER got into his ultimate blue rage as they both prepared for the combat.

Astrid and Oscar finally realized that they were using the wrong KAIJUNIZER weapon the whole time. Stephen then came into the basement, laughing at them for using the old technology-based KAIJUNIZER that was highly ineffective towards the kaijus.

"Oh Damn, that's why I couldn't get signals of their movements Oscar. This makes sense now. Well, if that's not THE REAL KAIJUNIZER then where is the real one," said Astrid as she felt stupid and curious. Oscar and Astrid were thinking about where THE REAL KAIJUNIZER could be located in the facility. Jeff turned on one of the news stations to get an update on the latest happenings around the city. "Guys look, we don't have time to argue about the kaijunizer right now, we have a bigger issue. Look at these wicked kaijus destroying our city! We need to stop them," said Jeff.

Oscar felt in his gut that Jeff knew where THE REAL KAIJUNIZER was located which was why he changed the subject. Astrid and Oscar knew something was off with Jeff like he was hiding THE REAL KAIJUNIZER somewhere in the base.

Elsewhere, STORM MONGA did a super loud roaring while sitting on top of a building with SPIDOTRON alongside her, while SERPO caused mayhem in New Orleans. In summary, Oscar thought after watching the news and hearing STORM MONGA'S Mighty Queen Roar that she could be causing the kaijus to go against the natural order.

"Whatever it is she wants with the kaijus is not good, this is why we should put our Faith/Hope in ROO KING to defeat her. He can beat her; I know he can. We are in the pandemic kaiju war now," said Oscar.

CHAPTER 3
Pandemic
The Kaiju War

As the night began, the pandemic kaiju war also began. Lots of bad things were happening in the magical and cultural city of New Orleans. Oscar was looking for a way to stop SPIDOTRON, SERPO, AND STORM MONGA from destroying the city.

The humans in New Orleans were terrified by the wicked kaijus that were wreaking havoc in the city and around the planet. The humans were looking to fight back against the villainous kaijus. Unfortunately, the villainous kaijus were winning super easily.

"I'm so sick of these bastards! We need to bring out the big missile that we've been working on for a decade now. No more playing it safe. It's time to kill these vindictive creatures!" said Stephen angrily.

"Sir, I don't think that's a good idea, you would just upset these antagonistic kaijus a lot more. I'm just looking out for you, this isn't the best solution to our situation," Jeff said, worried. Unfortunately, the big orange storm around New Orleans was getting bigger and stronger. Most homes were getting destroyed, while people were dying.

Fortunately, most humans were inside avoiding the storm even though they were very surprised by the humongous storm that was surrounding their homes and awesome city. Even still, humanity was on its knees in New Orleans, desperately needing a huge boost in Hope and Faith during the coronavirus pandemic and the surprising Kaiju Invasion.

Desperately looking for a Hero to restore the lost Hope and Faith that was once there. Fortunately, ROO KING blasts SPIDOTRON and STORM MONGA from a distance as he and THE LAKECRAWLER drew closer to their greatest enemies. Both were in their terrifying rages, ready for war.

THE LAKECRAWLER spat rounds of water from his mouth at SERPO from a distance. The news captured them from a helicopter from a distance as the war went on. Oscar, Tyrone, and Astrid watched and were very happy while everyone in New Orleans underestimated that THE LAKECRAWLER and ROO KING could defeat the villainous kaijus.

Lots of people were seriously sharing this doubt as ROO KING and his partner in crime, THE LAKECRAWLER, were outnumbered.

"ROO KING is a true underdog. He is perfect for the role to shock the non-believers who doubt him and that is how his power truly develops as an Omega Gladiator. So, keep counting him out fools hahaha," said Oscar with confidence.

"It's okay tho, I agree with you Oscar, haha. People need to stop underestimating ROO KING and especially that enormous blue lizard, THE LAKECRAWLER. They are going to shock the world," said Jeff with integrity.

SERPO also began spitting his red acid at THE LAKECRAWLER in his Red Rage of pure darkness. THE LAKECRAWLER ended up countering the attack with his own very special move.

At the outer parts of the light orange storm, SERPO and THE LAKECRAWLER collided and went to war. Likewise, SPIDOTRON with his boo-, STORM MONGA, were both watching ROO KING and vice versa. Staring at each other for a moment. Suddenly, ROO KING charged at them and went to war with his greatest enemies.

While the kaijus were battling it out, Tyrone, after fully charging his phone while being in the AOX Super Advanced Basement, went on Snapchat and texted a bunch of his crushes. Latinas he would like to date.

Unfortunately, some left him undelivered and then made posts, while others left him unread and then posted on the app. Tyrone felt depressed again so he got off the app and went back to watching his boy, ROO KING, kick some evil kaijus' asses.

When the lockdown took place back in March 2020, it made him super depressed and bored, like he didn't know if he was on the right path. He felt like he lost his motivation, inspiration, faith, and hope.

Fortunately, after seeing his new idols and favorite kaijus, ROO KING and THE LAKECRAWLER fight to kick the wicked kaijus asses not only did it give him life again but, it also gave him a chance at new hope and faith to build on for when life gets tough. To show warrior spirit and keep fighting no matter what. Tyrone was feeling a lot better since he saw ROO KING fighting.

However, SPIDOTRON got on top of ROO KING'S head trying to eat him while STORM MONGA got a good bite in. ROO KING was very hurt from the big bite again on his left arm, but he, fortunately, blasted SPIDOTRON with his Omega Beams at full speed and was forced to get him off of his head. SPIDOTRON was very weak and super hurt now as well. STORM MONGA was super angry after she saw her boo hurt and she went after ROO KING.

Amazingly, ROO KING jumped up very high and punched STORM MONGA super hard and fast with precision. Unfortunately, SPIDOTRON got back up and shot his acidic webs onto ROO KING, which made ROO KING start to feel very weak.

Tyrone then decided to go meet ROO KING, but Oscar decided it was way too dangerous for him to go alone. ROO KING ended up falling to the ground with draining energy.

STORM MONGA and SPIDOTRON continued to invade New Orleans and destroyed more of the city by unleashing chaos.

Fortunately, Tyrone and ROO KING soon ended up meeting.

Tyrone was very scared of him in person, but he was there to support him. He then encouraged him to get back up and save New Orleans and that he was The Ultimate King. "Let's geaux ROO KING! I know you are The Ultimate King. Go destroy them wicked monsters and save us. I know you can do it, big guy, I have faith and hope in you!" said Tyrone with some inspiration.

Unfortunately, THE LAKECRAWLER was down too, and hurt from SERPO'S deadly red acidic attacks. SERPO then went along with SPIDOTRON and STORM MONGA to continue invading NOLA.

However, Astrid and Jeff decided to team up and go to see THE LAKECRAWLER; and encouraged him to get back up and save humanity as well. ROO KING and THE LAKECRAWLER were both still down and hurt, but were regenerating so that they could bounce back and save the humans and city during the pandemic kaiju war.

"C'mon, big fella! I know you can heal and go destroy that stupid wicked black serpent, you got this," said Jeff with some encouragement to THE LAKECRAWLER.

Stephen and his military troops decided to fight the giant villainous monsters again by using their missiles. Unfortunately, STORM MONGA ate and destroyed the missiles with her mouth of storms, crushing them. Stephen was forced to pull out of the war. The rain and wind in the storm were getting stronger. Fortunately, THE LAKECRAWLER and ROO KING were regenerating but were still down.

While STORM MONGA, SERPO, and SPIDOTRON were out causing chaos and eating people, ROO KING and THE

LAKECRAWLER were getting stronger in their super-powerful regeneration power.

ROO KING and THE LAKECRAWLER were not going to relinquish their big war for humanity, or their favorite city from getting completely destroyed.

Next, THE LAKECRAWLER bounced back up stronger than ever to get back into the war and declared victory for not only New Orleans but all of humanity.

Jeff made a big connection with THE LAKECRAWLER and Astrid was very happy that her second most beloved creature was up ready for war. Likewise, ROO KING rose again and was also ready to bounce back by destroying his greatest enemies. Furthermore, ROO KING and Tyrone go up to each other in the rainy and windy street.

They make eye contact and they connect very deeply. They fist-bumped each other lightly and were both happy with connecting showing their ultimate warrior spirit.

THE LAKECRAWLER found ROO KING as Astrid and Jeff also found Tyrone and Oscar. They were all not only happy to reconnect as humans in the big storm but also how they could overcome adversity.

In fact, the humans were looking to get to safety by going inside a dark building to watch the storm get stronger while the wind and rain got more deadly.

On the bright side, ROO KING and THE LAKECRAWLER were ready to kick the villainous kaijus asses; to restore Hope and Faith to the humans in not only New Orleans but all of Louisiana. Although they were in a dark building, they ended up going to the top of the building to watch the kaiju war.

Incredibly, ROO KING and THE LAKECRAWLER stood side by side as STORM MONGA, SERPO, AND SPIDOTRON also stood side by side, looking at each other from a distance in the city before quickly charging at each other. Oscar, Astrid, Tyrone, and Jeff braced for the impact of the war alongside Stephen and his AOX Military troops. As a matter of fact, Stephen was searching for THE REAL KAIJUNIZER.

"Where the hell did I put That Real Kaijunizer? This kaiju pandemic war needs to seriously end dammit!" said Stephen.

Stephen was trying to figure out what happened with THE REAL KAIJUNIZER so he could possibly stop the kaiju pandemic war. On the other hand, Tyrone wanted to know why the kaijus were at war during the coronavirus pandemic. In fact, Tyrone came up with a very interesting theory.

"Wait a second, I just figured something out about the big kaiju pandemic war. What if the AOX Military is secretly controlling THE REAL KAIJUNIZER and using it to cause the kaijus to go to war?" said Tyrone with some curiosity.

Oscar and Jeff were really curious now too as to why this kaiju war just took place all of a sudden. They both thought that something was off and that the universe always had a way to bring the dark to the light. Oscar and Jeff both knew that the universe was going to bring the truth out one way or another. The REAL KAIJUNIZER was a super powerful advanced technological laptop that could even draw kaijus from outer worlds mysteriously and could cause lots of bad things to happen with the kaijus.

The kaijus were battling it out more brutally with some very gruesome attacks on each other. Unfortunately, no one knew where THE REAL KAIJUNIZER was located, not even Doctor Watkins and AOX owner, Stephen Hancock. As for the kaijus, they were going to war.

However, ROO KING stood mighty with his right fist in the air and interestingly enough in the city. As the giant storm was getting stronger, he mysteriously gained a new super ability with his fists becoming super powerful against his enemies, SPIDOTRON and STORM MONGA, while his ally THE LAKECRAWLER handled his other enemy SERPO for him. The kaiju pandemic war was very gruesome along with the storm being so big and strong.

While the kaijus were extremely powerful, the coronavirus seemed just as powerful as many people had, unfortunately, died from it in hospitals around the globe.

Moreover, a new virus called Variant (the coronavirus mutation) had hit Louisiana and was making vaccines ineffective due to its deadly power to overcome its obstacles.

Not like the kaijus, who also helped people around the globe to stay safe and be cautious of how deadly these viruses really were. Scientists were paying closer attention than ever to these deadly viruses in their labs to make sure people stayed safe when they were around other people and informing people on how to take care of themselves to prevent other people from possibly getting these viruses.

"Umm, I wonder if these kaijus are possibly carrying these viruses," said Jeff being curious. Oscar was really curious now too and was thinking about Jeff's idea.

As the pandemic kaiju war was going on, ROO KING quickly used his basic and special abilities to overcome adversity in the war of the space kaijus. THE LAKECRAWLER likewise, used his basic and special abilities to fight the giant wicked snake monster in a gruesome war. Matter of fact, Astrid began filming the big war and she saw some brutal attacks that could determine the outcome of the pandemic kaiju war. Lastly, something drastic and very chilling to the bone happened in the pandemic kaiju war that changed the outcome super quickly.

CHAPTER 4
Blood and War

The brutal bloody pandemic kaiju war continued. Midnight was filled with lots of kaijus' blood, splattered all over the buildings in New Orleans. The humans could not believe how gruesome this big war had become.

The kaijus were fighting to the death with some incredible amounts of durability, endurance, and stamina, while magically, the storm disappeared during the blood and war.

Stephen and his AOX Military Crew were making a secret weapon in another secret basement where they also created their weaponry. Elsewhere, Oscar, Astrid, and Tyrone were watching the war from a distance and they still couldn't believe the war was so brutal. The kaijus were true gladiators. Oscar believed these kaijus were true warriors in combat by how they were fighting to the death.

Astrid was still recording the kaiju bloody war. Suddenly, missiles started coming out of the blue at the kaijus, causing more blood to splatter.

New Orleans was a giant bloodbath filled with tons of blood. Having no more storms gave the AOX Military the advantage of taking out the kaijus. This time AOX was going to get their revenge for destroying the city that they fought to protect and also, beating them in battle back at Lake Pontchartrain.

"Time to kill these stupid animals! They don't belong here! Time to kill them once and for all to take back control over our city," said Stephen, declaring war with the kaijus from the AOX Facility. No matter the costs, he just wanted them to pay for their previous defeat in battle and at the same time, take back New Orleans so that they could rebuild it to help the citizens of the kaiju crisis.

"Sir, you are going to fight a losing war, they have not done anything to you. This is nature, of course, let them go to war. If you kill these kaijus, you will be doing New Orleans a disservice by possibly having other kaijus from around the globe come here and this time, humanity could go extinct. ROO KING AND THE LAKECRAWLER are fighting for humanity, they should not be killed!" said Oscar making it back to the AOX Facility to stop the war Stephen was causing from wiping out the gladiators.

"I don't care! These kaijus need to be killed to save my civilians in New Orleans, it's my job to protect them, Oscar," said Stephen in an angry tone.

Stephen was looking to find a way to eradicate the gladiators from existence in New Orleans but he was trapped because he could possibly kill lots, if not all, of the civilians in New Orleans.

"I mainly want to kill that stupid giant brown beast. That giant brown werewolf needs to die. I will destroy him one way or another," said Stephen with confidence. Oscar and Jeff were disappointed with Stephen's decision and his way of leading AOX, as a very shady company to society.

"Sir Oscar is right, killing these kaijus will be a huge mistake, especially ROO KING the giant brown beast. He truly is the king.

He can protect humanity and is more than capable of showing up in this pandemic kaiju war," said Astrid with faith in the kaijus/gladiators ROO KING and THE LAKECRAWLER.

The war was getting more intense as the AOX Military entered and brought big guns and bombs to destroy the kaijus. Surprisingly, the AOX Military was getting the best of the giant beasts with their newly designed weapons. As the kaijus were getting weaker, the AOX Military Troops were getting stronger with their tactics.

"ROO KING and THE LAKECRAWLER might be our best chance at survival, especially ROO KING since he can fight 2 gladiators and space kaijus at once. ROO KING could be our fighting chance at stopping other kaijus around the globe from coming here and destroying us and our city," said Tyrone. Jeff was thinking about Tyrone's empowering answer about ROO KING being the unstoppable force of destroying the other kaijus that could possibly come to Louisiana and cause chaos. Stephen was running out of options to end the kaijus.

"I'm getting ready to go destroy these kaijus, I've had enough of this nonsense. Doctor Watkins if something happens to me, I want you to run this company. It will be yours one hundred percent," said Stephen, getting ready to go to war in his big fighter jet, with a big missile that could possibly destroy the giant monsters.

Astrid, Tyrone, Oscar, and Jeff were looking at him and Doctor Watkins and weren't impressed.

"We need to stop him from destroying THE LAKECRAWLER and ROO KING. They are our last hope at surviving during this pandemic," said Astrid with integrity and faith. Oscar was thinking it through but he thought it would be wise for them to let him take a risk without interfering so he could learn his lesson.

There was a lot of blood from the kaijus on the ground and buildings from the pandemic kaiju war. The war was still going on with the AOX Military and Stephen involved, which could be a very deadly strategy that Stephen and his military were trying to execute.

AOX Military was now at war with the kaijus and was looking to cause more blood for the giant beasts. However, the government was not pleased with AOX's strategy for going to war with the kaijus.

They believed that going to war with the kaijus was a big mistake that would cost them a lot.

"This is a very bad idea. Stephen is going to seriously regret this decision," said Jeff with a very bad feeling. "You are right Jeff, I actually agree with you, this is not a good idea," said Doctor Watkins agreeing with Jeff.

Although Doctor Watkins respected Stephen's decision to interfere in the kaijus pandemic war, he still felt that it was a terrible idea. Doctor Watkins knew picking the wrong fight with these gigantic beasts could be a big risk, but worse it was something that Stephen couldn't come back from. Oscar and Jeff knew that this war was not Stephen's or AOX's.

The giant monsters were fighting back against AOX's fighter jets and were going beast mode on the jets by destroying them using their basic and special abilities. Oscar and everyone else was watching the war from the basement of the AOX Facility on AOX Super Advanced Smart TV on the news. Tyrone was very inspired by ROO KING'S and THE LAKECRAWLER'S abilities to come back from adversity to showcase their gladiator beast modes on their enemies.

STORM MONGA, ROO KING, and SPIDOTRON were destroying the AOX Fighter Jets. On the other hand, SERPO and THE LAKECRAWLER were really going to war on the other side of the city away from the blood and war in the Mississippi River.

Stephen was getting some really good gunshots on ROO KING amid the super brutal blood and war. In fact, ROO KING got wounded by the gunshots and immediately chased Stephen's fighter jet, but eventually missed surprisingly due to the buildings in his way.

Unfortunately for Stephen, he got hit by the Dark Orange Omega Beams from ROO KING, causing his fighter jet to go down very quickly. Something surprising happened after the jet crashed on the ground. Oscar, Doctor Watkins, and Jeff immediately ran to the crashed jet.

ROO KING made a big comeback in the war from constantly being jumped by SPIDOTRON and STORM MONGA. ROO KING brutally ripped off one of SPIDOTRON'S White Wings, hit him with his wings, and stabbed him in his back.

However, STORM MONGA powered up her fire tornadoes from her mouth at ROO KING, but he dodged and charged up his Green Electro-Lasers and brutally blasted STORM MONGA by destroying her with his special ability, which was more powerful than his normal Dark Orange Omega Beams. SPIDOTRON was still hurt on the ground from his big wound.

ROO KING was very angry at STORM MONGA who he immediately started grappling after blasting her with his super powerful Green Electro-Lasers. ROO KING ended up blasting at SPIDOTRON to make sure he didn't get back up. The war was now one versus one instead of two versus one with STORM MONGA getting weaker now that her big storms around New Orleans had disappeared.

Some of the AOX Military Troops were still alive and they had aborted the mission of destroying the kaijus to see where their leader was located. Oscar, Jeff, and Doctor Watkins were still running to the crash site as dawn was quickly approaching.

Astrid and Tyrone stayed behind to make sure that the security around the AOX Facility Lab was guaranteed. Tyrone ended up going on his Snapchat again.

He realized his other crush, Melanie, had blocked and ghosted him without any explanation. Moreover, Tyrone felt very hurt and was angry with how these Latin girls were treating him, he felt like giving up on his dream of Mexican Latina.

"Hey Tyrone, it's going to be okay. Forget that jerk, she doesn't deserve an awesome and handsome guy like you. The right Latina will come, don't worry," said Astrid.

Astrid tried to cheer him up again. Tyrone was still feeling down, he ended up going to the restroom filled with anger and confusion. Astrid ended up in cheers after seeing the kaijus battling it out at the end.

Tyrone quickly came back and became happy again seeing THE LAKE CRAWLER finish SERPO in a brutal fashion in the Mississippi River by the GNO Bridges after a long grueling war. On the other hand, STORM MONGA and ROO KING were still fighting it out in the city. It was very gruesome. Fortunately, ROO KING ended up finishing STORM MONGA with an incredibly powerful strike to save New Orleans and Louisiana in general by destroying the space monster in an epic finish strike. Finally, Oscar and the others found the jet, they immediately looked inside and were very shocked by the result.

CHAPTER 5
After War

Dawn has risen in New Orleans as it was destroyed by the gladiators. ROO KING did a very special and incredible strike that ended STORM MONGA to finish the pandemic kaiju war. SPIDOTRON was down and super hurt from ROO KING'S big strike that injured him. STORM MONGA flew away and SPIDOTRON followed her lead. Next, THE LAKECRAWLER was heading back to Lake Pontchartrain, his home from the war, to heal up and rest.

Suddenly, the News People were out on the streets from their News TV Station to record how damaged New Orleans was from the kaiju war and how humanity could finally come together to reunite, no matter what race, skin color, and/or ethnicity of humans.

"C'mon humanity, we need each other now more than ever. What happened to us being one Nation? We have been divided since Trump was in office, and we now officially have a new president fortunately . . . police y'all are supposed to protect us, but these last few years y'all failed at your jobs! Get the assholes out of their jobs by not just firing them but the death penalty as their punishment for killing innocent black people!" said News Anchor.

Since Joe Biden is now the new president, the future begins now with humanity coming together to finally end racism and police brutality, which is another very real issue in the USA that also needs to seriously end.

On the other hand, in the city there was an obstacle between the crashed jet, meanwhile, Oscar, Jeff, and Doctor Watkins were on one end looking to find a way to get on the other side.

The Jet was badly messed up from the outside; everyone except for Oscar was hopeful that Stephen was still alive if that was his jet. The news people were talking about the crash on the news stations.

Also, the news station talked about the giant brown beast known as ROO KING being the savior of the city. On the other hand, THE LAKECRAWLER got his praise as well.

Oscar and the others finally made it to the crashed jet; unfortunately, it was Stephen in the jet, so they immediately took him out to see if he was still alive.

ROO KING went to check him out as he did not mean to brutally attack the jet. However, Stephen didn't make it from the crash; everyone was sad except for Oscar. However, Jeff was only pretending to be sad even though he was glad that AOX was getting a new leader to help steer the company into The World's Greatest Kaiju Scientific/Military Base for understanding the kaijus.

The aftermath of the pandemic kaiju war was leaving a completely positive impact on society as ROO KING and THE LAKECRAWLER won their war to save and protect humanity from the dangers of The Colossal Space Gladiators that caused a lot of chaos on Earth from space.

"ROO KING left a big positive impact on the special and magical city of New Orleans for humanity," said Oscar with integrity.

Oscar felt proud to have such monstrous heroes like ROO KING and THE LAKECRAWLER saving the city and humanity during the pandemic, but the aftermath left lots of cleanups to do.

Fortunately, however, New Hope and Faith had been rebuilt and the humans felt they could grow together to make sure New Orleans became a much stronger and even more cultural city as time continued.

Not to mention, the aftermath of the pandemic kaiju war had also caused humanity to come together and stop looking at each other by Race, Skin Color, Nationality, etc., to finally come together as a species to become one and stop spreading hate and to start spreading more love and positivity.

Moreover, it also gets humans to become more humane and to practice more gratitude towards each other and in life. Hopefully, the aftermath will also teach police how to treat Black people with respect after years of violence.

Lots of changes occurred in NOLA after the enormous kaiju/gladiator war during the pandemic. Surprisingly, Louisiana's history in The Ultimate Kaiju History Book had lots of kaijus/gladiators going to battle and war.

Interestingly, a monstrous grey omega werewolf gladiator with electric fists was spotted in one of the pictures in the book battling it out with a creature from SPIDOTRON's and STORM MONGA's Species in the ancient days.

The kaijus, also known as Gladiators, possibly could have been at war since the 15th Century in Louisiana as the world was ancient with more mysteries being discovered in the giant monster's history. In the modern world, the history of the giant monsters could be resurfacing due to THE KAIJUNIZER controlling ROO KING and THE LAKECRAWLER, and The Space Monsters coming back to earth to possibly control SERPO and the other gladiators around the globe to rise, which caused them to collide in a big war.

"Wait a second, I think ROO KING and THE LAKECRAWLER were being controlled to fight and that SERPO the giant black snake was controlled as well," said Oscar with curiosity.

However, he just doesn't know what was controlling them to go to war.

"I think AOX and Stephen were controlling them. I feel like he had something to do with the war using THE REAL KAIJUNIZER," said Jeff.

"I strongly disagree with both of your opinions, these gladiators weren't being controlled. They sensed something was coming that was a huge threat to the world," said Doctor Andrew Watkins.

Mysteries began to rise as no one truly knew why ROO KING and THE LAKECRAWLER joined forces to fight in the pandemic kaiju war. Oscar, Doctor Watkins, and Jeff headed back to the facility.

On the other hand, Astrid and Tyrone were very happy that ROO KING and THE LAKECRAWLER won their wars, especially ROO KING saving the city against the 2 colossal, wicked space beasts.

After making it back to the Alpha/Omega X Gladiator Facility, Oscar ended up going into the lab to look at the Kaiju History book and came up with a theory. Astrid ended up coming into the lab to check on Oscar.

"Hey, are you okay, Oscar?? Just coming to check on you," said Astrid with Empathy.

"Hey, I'm okay thanks, Astrid, I just came up with a very interesting theory. I think in this book these are the same space creatures that have fought the silver-grey werewolf gladiator in the 15th century looking at this picture in this book, that might be ROO KING'S ancestor," said Oscar.

Oscar's very interesting theory hit close to home with the history of the gladiators going to war from ancient times; into the modern day with the pandemic kaiju war.

"Woah! That is a very interesting theory. Oscar, something has definitely hit the surface with this picture compared to the modern pandemic kaiju war," said Astrid, also curious. Astrid and Oscar didn't know ROO KING had an ancestor, which got more interesting. The truth was slowly coming out in The Ultimate Kaiju History Book. In fact, Alpha/Omega X has kept many of the secrets covered up for years from society, to not put fear in them to tell them giant monsters were real.

"Woah!! The LakeCrawler was once called The Ocean Reaper, cousins of and was once called The Lava Lizard Monster, a creature that lives in volcanoes, this got more interesting," said Oscar with more curiosity.

Oscar was thinking of what could have controlled ROO KING and THE LAKECRAWLER to fight and why the 2 Space Beasts had come to Earth; like their motive(s). Furthermore, he was also curious to know where THE REAL KAIJUNIZER was located in the Facility and how powerful it truly was that Stephen didn't mention.

Oscar knew that Stephen kept many secrets from him so he could protect his reputation for keeping Alpha/Omega X open and running. THE REAL KAIJUNIZER was a big mystery and could have been the cause of the pandemic kaiju war also causing the gladiators to collide.

Amazingly, lots of humans in New Orleans saw ROO KING walking towards the Mississippi River so he could head back to the swamp. Many people were creeped out, but others were very curious about his existence.

However, when ROO KING made it to the Mississippi River, he looked around at his favorite city, New Orleans, and howled like a true king to showcase he was the new king. The Ultimate King, ROO KING, went for a walk in the Mississippi River to make sure no other gladiator headed for New Orleans. Despite ROO KING being the new king, in a darkroom at AOX, THE REAL KAIJUNIZER was on silent mode and ended up spotting a Giant Egg in the Gulf of Mexico. Doctor Watkins ended up discovering THE REAL KAIJUNIZER; saw that there was a new Giant Egg in the Gulf of Mexico.

"What the hell is in that giant egg? Whatever it is, it's going to hatch soon so it will reveal itself," said Doctor Watkins very nervously.

Interestingly, the creature in the enormous egg in the middle of the Gulf of Mexico, in the after war, could be an UIC (UnIdentified Creature). Doctor Watkins is keeping a good eye on the enormous egg in the gulf.

"I wonder what is in that egg. This is very interesting. Maybe a new gladiator will be born," said Jeff in curiosity.

Jeff was curious to see what kind of creature was inside the enormous egg. THE REAL KAIJUNIZER was tracking what kind of species of the enormous creature was inside the egg.

Although, THE REAL KAIJUNIZER couldn't find what type of creature was inside the colossal egg. Furthermore, the data results that THE REAL KAIJUNIZER had pulled up stated that the gladiator (kaiju) living in the enormous egg was a UIC (UnIdentified Creature).

Not to mention, THE REAL KAIJUNIZER'S database had pulled up something very interesting. The enormous egg in the Gulf of Mexico was not from Earth due to its space-like appearance on the egg.

As for the city and humans of New Orleans, they were much more humbled and were willing to help each other from the pandemic kaiju war. Instead of seeing skin color and ethnicity within humanity, the humans felt like they had been divided thanks to a former stupid President Trump Sr, who caused the US to divide humanity by their ethnicities, skin color, and/or nationality.

Fortunately, ROO KING reminded humans to unite and conquer and to give humanity real hope and faith in what a true gladiator would do to protect his tribe. The humans in the after-war felt like they were finally reconnecting with their inner spirits to help them by rising above all hate like racism, police brutality, etc., of what Trump had caused within the country. ROO KING ended up coming back to the city.

"ROO KING provided us a new perspective of life and that is restoring Hope and Faith by being brave and conquering fear, he is a true king and monstrous hero," said Oscar with integrity and confidence.

Oscar gave hope to many people who may need to release negative energy and replace it with positive energy. Oscar truly believed ROO KING stood for Hope and Faith by replacing hate with love.

"You are so right Oscar, ROO KING truly is an inspiration for humanity in New Orleans and will soon be from around the globe," said Tyrone with enthusiasm.

Tyrone found his new inspiration; he felt so happy and much more alive about the positive impact ROO KING had made on him. On the other hand, Astrid and ROO KING had a deep love connection. Incredibly, Astrid's and ROO KING'S energies matched romantically.

Eventually, ROO KING had Astrid in his massive powerful hands; Astrid was very scared of heights, but she had faith that he wouldn't drop her. ROO KING decided to bring her home on a nice warm night in his enormous hands, surprisingly, he knew where she lived.

ROO KING showed compassion for humanity despite the hatred many people had in their hearts toward him. He felt very sad that he was rejected by society because he was a giant monster and that he couldn't be a hero because he was an enormous monster.

Society doesn't like giant monsters, but ROO KING is very motivated to end the discrimination from society against giant monsters because he is not a bad monster.

Fortunately, Tyrone and ROO KING ended up connecting in the city; they both were very motivated as a team to prove their doubters wrong for even hating them, to get them to hate them more. Tyrone and ROO KING knew evil never wins. Lots of changes were being made in New Orleans. After the pandemic kaiju war, teaching everyone to be more appreciative, and to show more love and positivity instead of hate and negativity.

In fact, many people in New Orleans were scared of ROO KING but they truly respected him, even though they had others who just didn't like him and wanted him dead for good unfortunately. The city of New Orleans midtown and uptown were really back to rebuilding mode but with New Hope/Faith being reborn for the better.

"People including the police need to stop spreading hate and negativity; start being more appreciative by showing more love and positivity towards each other. We are all humans, screw race, skin color, nationality, and ethnicity; those are just labels," said Astrid with encouragement.

Astrid truly thought humans should stick together no matter what, stop trying to tear each other down and start uplifting each other more to make Earth a much better place. Deep down inside Astrid knew that this world was a very dark and scary place to live, but she truly believed that humanity could come together if they wanted and if they were in a super scary event like the pandemic kaiju war.

The gladiators also knew that the kaijus were put on this planet for a reason, and the reason they were on this planet was a good mystery to be solved as to why they had risen back up. Doctor Andrew Watkins was looking to make changes to AOX Facility by using THE REAL KAIJUNIZER to continue tracking the kaijus (gladiators), but studying more into their origins of the gladiators, and also studying the anatomy of their bodies and more about their abilities.

Doctor Watkins was looking to study a lot more on the gladiators, not just their origins and abilities but also their habitats and histories. Next, Doctor Watkins wasted no time on THE REAL KAIJUNIZER to find out the different kaijus that had risen all of a sudden; the space gladiators such as STORM MONGA and SPIDOTRON, of what planet they were from, and what caused them to invade Earth.

Many theories were possible according to Doctor Watkins even though Jeff and Oscar wanted to find out about the glad-iators as well.

"Wow there are over 10 kaijus rising up including THE LAKECRAWLER, ROO KING, SPIDOTRON, and STORM MONGA this just got a lot more interesting," said Doctor Watkins.

Moreover, Doctor Watkins discovered the different kaijus that had risen from around the world. Amazingly, Jeff and Oscar saw that the seismic charges that the enemies possessed were forces to be reckoned with. As a matter of fact, Oscar and Jeff discovered that the kaijus, even THE LAKECRAWLER, and ROO KING were evolving. "This is incredible, they are evolving and adapting more and more each day.

"The Kaijunizer is tracking their evolution. Wow this really is sophisticated," said Jeff.

Jeff was totally amazed by the evolution of the kaijus (gladiators) of which some were still growing. The kaijus were becoming more modernized as they were becoming more extravagant in their DNA according to THE REAL KAIJUNIZER.

"As Earth is becoming more modernized and advanced, same with the kaijus they are adapting and evolving with the planet to become more revolutionized, this is just astonishing," said Oscar.

According to Oscar, he truly believed that the more Earth was being modernized, the more the kaijus were adapting and evolving along with the planet which was spectacular. Not to mention, the kaijus could be gaining new abilities as they adapted and evolved.

AOX Jeff and Oscar truly thought these giant beasts were gaining new basic and possibly special abilities. THE KAIJUNIZER was picking up on the new abilities of each giant beast in a very interesting 4D image of each profile for each kaiju on the computer's super-advanced screen. THE KAIJUNIZER finally picked up information on the mysterious monstrous black egg in the Gulf of Mexico; the colossal black egg looked like an enormous space rock with some green lines on the outside of the egg. AOX was looking to study the colossal black/green egg in the Gulf of Mexico.

"Woah! The seismic activity we are getting from this humongous egg is most certainly not from Earth by the sound of the creature that is in that egg; the seismic sounds a lot like Storm Monga interestingly," said Oscar.

Oscar was starting to have a very interesting theory of what the creature inside of the egg could be. Many theories could play into a big factor in what type of monster could be living inside of the humongous space egg.

"I have a strange feeling this giant beast is going to be the daughter of Storm Monga and Spidotron which could be the reason why Storm Monga is so aggressive and why she came to Earth because Earth is their best chance at survival from their homeworld," said Oscar with confidence.

Oscar was not too sure, but he was confident that STORM MONGA and SPIDOTRON chose Earth as the birthplace of their newborn baby kaiju to be born at. Surprisingly, the Gulf of Mexico was STORM MONGA'S and SPIDOTRON'S new home so they could protect their kaiju baby from any possible enemies.

"Wait a second Oscar, so you think that enormous and ferocious worm-eating monster and that super giant and weird-looking spider have a baby together, I'm sorry but that is hard to believe," said Jeff in disagreement with Oscar.

Jeff truly believed that didn't sound right to him; he felt he needed some evidence in order to agree with Oscar. Doctor Watkins was doing more research on the giant baby kaiju inside the Colossal Space Egg. In fact, Doctor Watkins might have evidence that Oscar was right.

"Guys come see this, Oscar was right but turns out the creature inside one of the eggs that belongs to STORM MONGA and SPIDOTRON, this could lead to a global war if we are not careful," said Doctor Watkins.

According to THE REAL KAIJUNIZER, it proved that inside

the colossal egg were STORM MONGA'S and SPIDOTRON'S babies because the DNA from the super advanced laptop collected a lot of information on the new giant creature.

On the other hand, ROO KING was standing like an Ultimate King, looking out for his territory and ready for anything to come his way. He watched from the swamp, looking at the lake and New Orleans with his fists balled up ready for more battles and wars. Interestingly, the monstrous egg in the Gulf of Mexico ended up hatching.

THE REAL KAIJUNIZER ended up tracking the creature; it was a very odd-looking and very aggressive giant monster. Lastly, another colossal Space Egg was found just outside of the Louisiana coastline; unfortunately, THE REAL KAIJUNIZER somehow did not track this one.

CHAPTER 6
Rise of the Ultimate King

On a tropical summer dawn, the giant brown beast transformed into the humans now called The Ultimate King, ROO KING, rose, and watched over the swamp. Unfortunately, from out of nowhere, SERPO came back and brutally attacked him from behind on his right shoulder.

ROO KING was super angry and immediately attacked back; fortunately, GLADIUS ROO was able to get him off of his right shoulder. AOX and Astrid were watching the rematch from the lab as Jeff and Oscar were very familiar with the 1st fight.

"Oh, snap SERPO really sees ROO KING as a huge threat to his so-called claimed kingdom, this is a spiteful rematch from SERPO, he doesn't like ROO KING," said Oscar. Amazingly, Oscar finally realized there was some kind of lowkey rivalry between SERPO and ROO KING that they were unaware of. ROO KING didn't like SERPO either.

"This rematch is not just about them being rivals, but it's about who is the more powerful gladiator to see who the true king of the swamp is, this is getting very fascinating," said Jeff.   According to Jeff, the rematch could be more than just a rivalry between ROO KING and SERPO in the swamp, it could be to see who the real king of the swamp was. ROO KING and SERPO rivalry was heating up but they were still growing as THE REAL KAIJUNIZER tracked their growth in the AOX Scientist Lab.

"Wait a second, they both are fully grown, but are still growing according to the Ultanium still in the swamp. It seems like it's not going away any time soon, which means SERPO and ROO KING are still growing from the Ultanium. This is insane," said Doctor Watkins.

It turned out that the two colossal beasts were somehow still growing. The kaijus were getting trickier and more complex as time went on, especially with their heights.

AOX knew that the smartest, strongest, and most powerful gladiators that were going to survive in the modern world as the gladiators, evolved more than ever in 2021 which could be why the kaijus including SERPO and ROO KING, and possibly THE LAKECRAWLER, were still growing rapidly even though they were fully grown.

In the new year 2021, the gladiators were looking to become more powerful and explosive as if they knew something big was coming to the planet, possibly like a global war. Although ROO KING was fully grown at 346 feet and was halfway to his real height yet by surprise, he had so much love for Astrid Rodriguez as far as his romantic interest was concerned. Not to mention, ROO KING'S Dark Orange Omega Beams were just developing as he was getting older.

On the other hand, in New Orleans on a special Friday Afternoon . . . Tyrone went out for coffee to help clear his mind from other girls who brutally and mentally hurt him in his dark romantic past. After walking into the coffee shop and buying his coffee he ended up seeing one super gorgeous Mexican-Hispanic Girl that looked his age. She was in the coffee shop on her laptop.

Tyrone looked her way and when she looked back at him, he quickly turned his head. He tried to decide if he should approach her. He was super nervous and was crushing on her very hard. He decided to just let go of his fear and have the courage to approach a crush he likes very well.

"Hi there, my name is Tyrone, you look so astonishing like the stars in the galaxy haha," said Tyrone with some confidence.

"Hi Tyrone, it's a pleasure to meet you, haha, my name is Brenda," said Brenda with a glorious smile.

Tyrone was stunned and happy that he made his approach. "It's a pleasure to meet you Brenda, I couldn't resist your charm from a distance that's been lighting my day up haha, would you be down to go on a coffee date sometime?" asked Tyrone with confidence.

Brenda was quite shocked and loved his confidence. "Wow! I can't believe you were so brave and sweet to come up to meet me and ask me out, without being rude like other guys. I would love to go out with a handsome guy like you haha, that's a yes btw," said Brenda with joy.

Tyrone was super excited within his spirit as he finally got to go on a date with his crush. Brenda and Tyrone were laughing while getting to know each other at the coffee shop.

Meanwhile, back at the swamp, the colossal fight was very brutal between the two extremely powerful gladiators; SERPO and ROO KING. Unfortunately, ROO KING was losing badly to SERPO this time.

Astrid went to Treasure Chest to cheer on her lover, a giant brown beast, to win. Matter of fact, ROO KING and SERPO were fighting just on the lake coast of the casino called Treasure Chest in Kenner. Oscar ended up going with Astrid to make sure she was safe during the big battle.

"I refuse to see my enormous brown beast lose to that wicked black serpent creature again," said Astrid.

AOX was watching to make sure no more kaijus (gladiators) or space gladiators appeared out of nowhere in the stratosphere to invade the big battle. Sergeant Jeff Curtman was the new leader of the Alpha/Omega X military squad, and he had his big weapons on standby in case any space gladiator decided to appear in the stratosphere to interfere in the ROO KING \SERPO big battle.

Doctor Watkins was watching the battle carefully from THE REAL KAIJUNIZER. Sergeant Curtman and his AOX Military troops were prepared for war with their weapons intact for anything to come their way in New Orleans. Sergeant Curtman had been preparing his troops since the rise of the kaijus around the globe, especially in Louisiana. On the other hand, Tyrone was walking his new date, Brenda, home from the coffee shop; they were talking about dating each other.

"I couldn't resist meeting a true special queen like you; I'm so glad I came up to talk to you. I can't wait to date you, Brenda," said Tyrone with joy and confidence.

"Awww how sweet you are and a very handsome guy, Tyrone. Anyone that treated you wrong doesn't know what they lost, you are a chosen one, you may be the right guy for me," said Brenda with pure joy and happiness.

Brenda and Tyrone were very happy talking to each other, and both felt the same way romantically. They ended up exchanging phone numbers and Snapchats to contact each other. Next, Tyrone went home and chilled on the couch and turned on the TV, he ended up seeing the news. The news showed the rematch of ROO KING and SERPO battling it out on the lake coast by Treasure Chest in Kenner. Tyrone ended up getting hyped up and cheering for his boy ROO KING to kick SERPO'S ass in the rematch.

"Ayeee c'mon ROO you got this, whoop his ass, let's go," said Tyrone while cheering for his favorite kaiju/gladiator ROO KING.

Astrid and Oscar made it to the big battle scene. ROO KING and SERPO were duking it out like kings on the lake coast. Unfortunately, ROO KING was down and saw Astrid and Oscar from a distance. Astrid went up to him to connect with him in his downfall.

"C'mon ROO KING, you got this my favorite giant beast! You can do this. Rise back up and destroy him, you are our savior GLADIUS ROO," said Astrid with Hope and Warrior Spirit. Astrid encouraged ROO KING to get back up and defeat SERPO to claim the swamp.

"Astrid you may want to get back here, SERPO is launching out of the lake water coming our way," said Oscar.

Astrid saw SERPO and headed back to the shore to meet Oscar. SERPO was quickly heading for them by flying towards them viciously. As SERPO flew quicker towards them, Astrid and Oscar stayed still; SERPO inched closer to them.

Fortunately, ROO KING grabbed SERPO by his tail and swung/threw him back into the lake. "RAWWWRR" super loud noise by ROO.

ROO KING roared at him from a distance to protect a couple of his favorite humans. ROO KING looked at Astrid and Oscar to connect with them; they looked at him too; they also were cheering for him to win. SERPO was quickly charging at ROO KING roaring too. However, SERPO started spitting his red acid again. Likewise, ROO KING fired back at SERPO with his Omega Beams. They ended up hitting each other with their powers, it was a very close and grueling battle.

"C'mon ROO KING kick that bastard ass, you got this big fella," said Doctor Watkins watching from his Alpha/Omega X lab.

Tyrone was still hyping while cheering for ROO KING from home on the news on TV, even though he and his new date, Brenda, were texting each other about their future dates.

In the middle of the battle, ROO KING threw rocks at SERPO, unfortunately, they were not hurting him from a distance. Furthermore, they ended up charging at each other in the shallow part of the lake; they brutally started attacking each other with their devastating blows to possibly end the battle. Astrid and Oscar got back at a farther distance from the colossal battle.

The battle in the lake was very grueling with the gladiators throwing down, it was a very tough bloody battle. SERPO was now unleashing a battle-finishing move which was his super deadly red acidic breath, as he got ROO KING where he wanted him in the lake. Astrid and Oscar were very nervous about ROO KING.

On the other hand, Tyrone at home was getting upset with watching the battle on TV.

"ROO KING lookout, you got this please don't let me down big guy ugh, please destroy that stupid giant black snake," said Tyrone as he was getting frustrated with SERPO.

Tyrone was carefully watching the battle and was hoping for his monstrous hero ROO KING to win. He had faith in him to get the win.

As the battle began to end, SERPO ended up blasting ROO KING with his super deadly red acidic breath, unfortunately, ROO was feeling very weak and he was very drained from the red acidic breath. Adversity was getting bigger and tougher for ROO KING. SERPO was looking like the ultimate king as far as who the true king was, unfortunately. Astrid started crying; Oscar was very nervous about ROO KING.

"Nooo get up ROO KING, please we need you, we know you are the ultimate king. Please do it for us, you can handle adversity and anything that comes your way ROO KING, you are a king we truly have faith in you," said Astrid in tears.

ROO KING ended up facing the water secretly healing up to regain his energy. SERPO was going after Astrid and Oscar by using red acidic spits; the humans were cornered by a dead end in the park.

Moreover, SERPO ended up closing in on them; the spectacular comeback happened as ROO KING rose in his Green Rage. He immediately grabbed SERPO'S tail again, but this time with his true strength and brute force. ROO KING ended up wrestling with him and lit him up with his Dark Green Electro-lasers in full force this time on land. SERPO was hurt and now very weak. ROO KING unleashed his inner giant beast and destroyed SERPO by punching him at full speed while using his ultimate agility, peak intelligence, lightning-fast reflexes, and unlimited stamina to keep him in the battle.

SERPO'S super durability, flight, mobility, and stealth were no doubt incredible which kept him from taking ROO KING'S super precise, very fast, really hard, and super powerful strikes (scratches, punches, elbows, and slaps). Vice versa with ROO KING taking lots of SERPO'S bites and tail whips. Astrid and Oscar were both super excited about ROO KING'S huge comeback.

"Look, Oscar, he has healed and he's ready to destroy this stupid serpent, let's go ROO KING we knew you could do it, whoop that bastard's ass," said Astrid with hope and faith.

Oscar was smiling very widely as his buddy made a big comeback.

Likewise, Tyrone was super excited that his buddy made a big comeback to destroy the colossal black serpent gladiator. ROO KING was absolutely destroying SERPO with full rage using his Green Electro-lasers to level up.

"Damn ROO KING, I didn't know you could do that, this is incredible, get him big guy," said Oscar, amazed by his Green Electro-lasers.

Jeff and Doctor Watkins were very excited about ROO KING'S big comeback to help him stop the enormous/ferocious serpent to protect humanity.

"This is very insane. I didn't know he had that extraordinary special ability," said Jeff.

Doctor Andrew Watkins was also surprised but he knew besides Oscar that ROO KING was a very special gladiator. "Never know what he is capable of, never underestimate a giant special beast like him. Anyways, I think he has more special abilities that we still don't know about," said Doctor Andrew Watkins.

Next, back at Treasure Chest's Lake Coast, ROO KING was going for his final move to destroy SERPO. ROO KING blasted SERPO'S head off his neck and body for the kill and defeated the giant swamp black serpent beast. "OWOOOOO" the loud howl from The Ultimate King in his victory, although it was in the daytime again like the first battle.

Lots of people were watching him and vice versa, but the humans, besides Astrid and Oscar, were very scared of him. Surprisingly, some people clapped for ROO KING after his victory; he had inspired the people who clapped for him and showed them a new way of Hope and Faith in adversity, no matter what life threw their way. ROO KING was back to his normal self and he was happy with the people he inspired. He felt like a true hero in kaiju form.

Astrid and ROO KING went up together; he held her in his hands as they loved each other, while Oscar and ROO KING looked at each other. They went about their business although they were happy with each other. Oscar finally drove back to the Alpha/Omega X Lab to meet Astrid and ROO KING there. Oscar knew Astrid was in very good hands.

However, ROO KING and Astrid were on the news as he walked to New Orleans with his love interest in his massive hands.

Tyrone on the other hand was super excited his favorite beast won the big battle rematch between his foe. The WWL-TV news people couldn't believe ROO KING existed. They were blown away; due to the kind of creature he was and especially his monstrous size of a beast he was.

Doctor Watkins and Jeff were very proud of ROO KING for getting his third victory. ROO KING was giving lots of hope to humans during the pandemic, even though the news people were still talking about how the coronavirus was getting worse.

"This suck badly and I'm getting sick of wearing these stupid masks, I wish ROO KING could wipe out every coronavirus from around the world, so our planet can go back to the real normal and not this fake normal," said Jeff with some anger.

Jeff was concerned that everyone could be wearing masks even until 2022; he was certainly getting frustrated from COVID-19.

"As far as scientists are saying, we may still need to wear masks in 2022, although the vaccines are now out. A new Virus named Delta Variant is getting more deadly and the coronavirus is getting more dangerous in California.

"Everyone, please stay safe, please wash your hands, avoid large gatherings, and mask up," said Anchor Sally Whitmore.

The news anchor, Sally, told everyone to be safe and how the Coronavirus Delta variant was becoming more dangerous in California.

"Wow! This is getting ridiculous with this stupid virus; face mask BS we need this virus to go away I have faith it will end soon, hopefully before 2022," said Tyrone as he was still watching the news on WWL-TV.

Tyrone was getting tired of the pandemic. He was sad and hoped he and his new possible girlfriend, Brenda can still go on their dates. Likewise, Brenda hoped the same way because she was so glad to have met an awesome guy like Tyrone. Unfortunately, cases of the Coronavirus and Delta Variant were skyrocketing all over the world, not just in the USA.

Everyone around the globe was looking for that big hope to believe in to help them get through this deadly pandemic. Something had already been given during the midst of this pandemic; that was ROO KING existing to give humanity a restoration of New Hope and Faith to help them get through COVID-19.

ROO KING was surprisingly a big miracle during the pandemic, doing his best to connect with humans and spread light in their darkest times. Fortunately, society was beginning to see ROO KING was not evil, but a hero, not just any hero though, a MONSTROUS HERO who was being misunderstood and underappreciated and who wanted to be loved as well.

The NOLA Government was very surprised that ROO KING'S connection to humanity was actually spreading light and positivity while he was helping humans to better cope with the viruses that were popping up and unfortunately killing others. Doctor Watkins was watching the news and was very happy and touched by ROO KING doing his best to connect with humans during the pandemic as he was walking back to New Orleans with his love interest Astrid in his very massive hands.

"He truly is our last hope and faith in this dark pandemic because he really is THE ULTIMATE KING," said Doctor Watkins with so much joy and inspiration.

Doctor Watkins already had his New Hope, Faith, and Inspiration in his monstrous idol ROO KING of how he was spreading love, light, and positivity to humans during these tough times. Many humans were beginning to see that ROO KING really was a hero and not just a monster that was causing destruction during the pandemic.

In fact, society had proved that they had discriminated against the giant brown beast. Humanity was on its knees unfortunately, due to the coronavirus pandemic that had caused chaos since it launched back in March 2020, when the lockdown first started. Since the pandemic started back in March 2020, the world has not been the same.

"This world is not going to be the same as pre-covid. Once post-covid hits this truly sucks," said Oscar with frustration.

As COVID-19 was getting worse and worse in 2021, Trump was no longer the US President anymore, and somehow the viruses magically disappeared before 2022. Oscar was getting sick of the pandemic and just wanted life to go back to the real normal.

The world was changing in the world of COVID-19; sadly back in 2020 lots of people despite race and ethnicity had died. Likewise, in 2021 it was very unfortunate that many people were still dying as COVID-19 was getting worse. Oscar was driving towards New Orleans and saw ROO KING from a distance walking towards the city as he had his love interest in his hands very safely. Moments later, they made it back to the Alpha/Omega X Facility; ROO put Astrid down on the ground safely and truly connected with her spiritually. Oscar was getting close as he was now in the city driving to the AOX Facility in the afternoon.

"Yess, I knew you were the greatest hero ROO KING, my favorite colossal beast, you are really awesome," said Tyrone McStevens with joy.

Tyrone was so honored to have his favorite kaiju ROO KING spreading love, inspiration, hope, faith, and positivity to humanity in these dark and tough times in the now COVID-19 World as he was still watching WWL-TV News.

"These viruses do not want no smoke with my super monstrous hero ROO KING in a global war, he'll destroy these viruses with his extremely powerful Omega Beams," said Tyrone McStevens.

Tyrone had a lot of faith, confidence, and pride that ROO KING would absolutely destroy the coronavirus in a big all-out war.

Astrid and ROO were connecting before he went for a walk back to the swamp or the Mississippi River in the city. Oscar pulled up and made it back to the Facility by seeing Astrid and ROO KING connecting with each other romantically and spiritually.

Oscar was very happy to see them both, and vice versa as they all had a positive and loving connection with each other as living beings even though Astrid and ROO were lovers. Interestingly, ROO KING and Oscar made their connection emotionally and physically in different ways with their facial expressions eye to eye contact. Oscar and the monstrous brown werewolf gladiator king connection was very powerful as they both displayed dominance in their physical bond.

In fact, Oscar and ROO KING showed how powerful a bond can be between a man and a colossal terrifying-looking beast.

Lastly, THE REAL KAIJUNIZER went off by surprise in the lab; Jeff found some terrifying information on the new baby kaijus were hatching, and some new frightening kaijus were now rising from the swamp where ROO KING lived, a global war could be coming sooner than expected.

In summary, the Monstrous Hero must do everything within his power to stop The Space Monsters from taking over the planet.

About the Author

Ray Synigal is a super entertainment fanatic from the Bayou region of New Orleans, Louisiana. Ray's main passion is writing classic, fresh, new, and original Sci-Fi giant monster stories. Synigal's true love for his Sci-Fi Kaiju movies, comics/graphic novels, and/or short kaiju fiction stories has inspired Ray to create his own Sci-Fi Kaiju stories. Not to mention, to add to his main passion before graduating high school back in May 2017 in Georgia, he won a mini Oscar Award from his Audio/Video Tech class. Ray is now back in Louisiana with his parents, and 3 younger siblings, where he continues to write his first-ever book series to launch his Author career.